W9-APK-994

Hillel Builds A House

by
Shoshana Lepon

illustrated by
Marilynn Barr

KAR-BEN COPIES, INC.   ROCKVILLE, MD

LIBRARY OF CONGRESS
Library of Congress Cataloging-in-Publication Data

Lepon, Shoshana
    Hillel builds a house / Shoshana Lepon; illustrated by Marilynn Barr
        p.   cm.
    Summary: A young boy who loves to build houses learns that the perfect holiday for him is Sukkot.
        ISBN 0-929371-41-0:   ISBN 0-929371-42-9 (pbk.):
    (1.   Fasts and feasts—Judaism—Fiction. 2. Sukkot—Fiction. 3. House construction—Fiction. 4.
Jews—United States—Fiction.) I. Barr, Marilynn ill. II. Title.
PZ7.L5555H1   1993
(E)—dc20   92-39383
CIP
AC

Text copyright © 1993 by Shoshana Lepon
Illustrations copyright © by Marilynn Barr
All rights reserved. No portion of this book may be reproduced without the written permission of the publisher.
Published by KAR-BEN COPIES, INC., Rockville, MD 1-800-4-KARBEN
Printed in the United States of America

*To all the children
of the Diaspora Yeshiva Day School
and especially to Yosef,
who likes to build houses.*
                    —S.L.

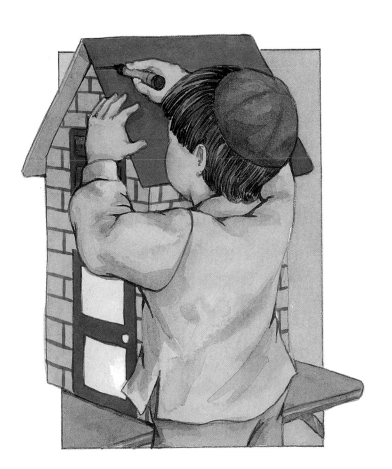

"Where is Hillel?" his father asked. "I haven't seen him all afternoon. It's time to light the Hanukkah candles."

"In his room," answered his mother. "He must be building another house."

Hillel *was* building another house.

He loved to build houses.

Last summer, it was a tree house in the old oak out back.

When the days got chilly, Hillel made a new house under the basement steps.

Now even the basement was too cold. Hillel dragged a large carton upstairs to his room. This would be his winter house.

His parents found Hillel in the carton. He was setting up his menorah.

"I'm going to celebrate Hanukkah in my new house!" Hillel declared.

"Your house is great," said his mother. "But you can't light candles in it."

"Why not?" asked Hillel.

"Because you might start a fire," his mother answered. "Besides, we light the menorah in the window so everyone will know about the miracle of Hanukkah."

Hillel moved his menorah down to the living room.

"Next holiday," he said to himself, "I'll celebrate in my very own house!"

Soon it would be Purim.

Hillel's friends were going to dress up in costume. They would go from house to house and give out baskets of treats called shalach manot.

Hillel thought and thought. Suddenly he had an idea.

He would not stay at home in his house. He would take his house outside with him. He would dress up as a house for Purim!

Hillel cut and glued and painted. At last his costume was ready.

A pointy red roof rested on his head. There were small windows in front for his eyes, and bigger windows at the sides for his arms.

On Purim morning, Hillel got up early. He put on his house and hurried outside.

He could not see the sky overhead.
He could not see the dark clouds.
But he could feel the raindrops.

Soon his house was a mess of soggy cardboard!

Hillel ran home to change. He put on the space suit he had worn last year. He put his raincoat over it, and went back outside.

"Next holiday...," he sighed.

The next holiday was Passover.

Hillel was excited. He went from room to room, gathering all the pillows he could find. He piled them into a snug little fort. "I'll play in here the whole week of Passover," he decided.

But his mother thought differently.

"Hillel," she said, "you have to take your house apart. We're having lots of guests, and we need the pillows. At the seder we lean back like kings to show that we are free!"

Hillel took the pillows down and handed them to his mother. "Next holiday…," he whispered to himself.

Spring had arrived. It was warm and sunny outside.

Hillel tied some old sheets together and raised them on a pole in the backyard. He took out his sleeping bag.

"Tonight is Shavuot," he said. "I'll sleep out under the stars. I'll be like the Jews in the desert, when they got the Torah at Mt. Sinai."

"You won't be sleeping here, tonight, Hillel," said his father, peeking into the tent. "In fact you won't be sleeping at all. Tonight we go to synagogue. We stay up all night and study Torah. This year you're old enough to come along."

Hillel was excited. He had never stayed up all night!

He gave his house one last look.

"Next holiday...," he promised.

On Rosh Hashanah, Hillel sat quietly beside his father in the synagogue. He liked the songs. But the prayers were long, and Hillel was getting tired.

He snuggled down in his seat and pulled one end of his father's tallit over his head. It made a nice little house.

Hillel put his prayer book down. He would just rest his eyes for a minute....

"Hillel! Hillel!" his father shook him gently. "Wake up! It's time to hear the shofar."

Hillel peered out from under the tallit.

Rosh Hashanah was no time for sleeping.

And it was no time for houses.

Yom Kippur was no time for houses, either. Hillel didn't need anyone to tell him that.

He would not fast all day like the grown-ups, but he would go to synagogue. And he would try to follow along in his prayer book.

When Hillel got home from synagogue, the sky was filled with stars.

"Come, Hillel," said his father. "Get a flashlight. I want you to help me."

Hillel followed his father out to the tool shed.

"Shine the light up here," said his father. "I have to take down some boards."

"What do you need boards for?" asked Hillel.

"Don't you know what the next holiday is?" his father asked. "It's Sukkot! It's time to start building our sukkah. For seven days we'll eat outside under the stars, like the Jews who came out of Egypt."

"Sukkot!" exclaimed Hillel. "How could I have forgotten? Sukkot means hammers and nails and branches and fruits and lots of decorations."

"Sukkot is the perfect time to build a house!"

GLOSSARY

Hanukkah	The Festival of Lights, commemorates the Jewish victory over Syrian King Antiochus.
Menorah	Eight-branched candelabra lit during Hanukkah.
Passover	Festival celebrating the Jewish exodus from Egypt.
Purim	Holiday celebrating the victory of the Jews over evil Haman.
Rosh Hashanah	The Jewish New Year.
Seder	Traditional Passover meal.
Shalach Manot	Baskets of sweet treats shared among friends on Purim.
Shavuot	Holiday celebrating Moses receiving the Ten Commandments.
Shofar	Ram's horn, blown on Rosh Hashanah.
Sukkah	Harvest booth, built during Sukkot.
Sukkot	Fall harvest holiday.
Tallit	Prayer shawl.
Torah	First five books of the Bible.
Yom Kippur	Day of Atonement.